Easy Gospel Songs
for the
Harmonica
Volume 1

80+ Gospel Tunes You Can Play Today!

Howdy!

I am so glad you decided to buy this collection of Easy Gospel Songs for the Harmonica: Volume 1.

One of my greatest joys is to see people who have never even picked up a harmonica before begin playing songs that they love.

And who doesn't love gospel tunes?

So, enjoy.

Play often and get ready. You'll soon become addicted to the persuasive power of the harmonica.

I hope it makes you happy and brings a smile to those listening to you play.

Enjoy!

Clint

How to Use This Book

Before I tell you how to use this book, let me tell you a secret on playing the harmonica.

OK, come closer.

Here it is.

There is no right or wrong way to play the harmonica.

In fact, there are almost as many harmonica styles as there are harmonica players.

So how will you know if you're doing it the right way?

You need to spend time with your harp.

Preferably, you need to play it every day. I'd recommend at the very least 10 minutes a day.

Get a feel for it. Get to know how she likes to be played, how she works.

Only then will you be able to develop your own style of harmonica playin'.

OK, now back to this book.

There are over 80 gospel harmonica songs included in the book. Each song includes notes and lyrics. However, additionally, each song contains harmonica tablature.

If this is your first time playing the harmonica, it's likely you've never encountered this type of tablature before (tablature is just a fancy word for a system to make it easier to read and play music).

Harmonica tablature for the C harmonica is made up of the numbers 1 through 10. Each number corresponds to the numbered holes on a basic diatonic harmonica.

And each hole on a C harmonica corresponds to two separate notes:

	1	2	3	4	5	6	7	8	9	10
Blow	C	E	G	C	E	G	C	D	G	C
Draw	D	G	B	D	F	A	B	E	F	A

If you've spent more than 2 seconds with a harmonica, you know that you can both blow and draw each hole.

So, there's got to be a way to know whether you should blow or draw, right?

Luckily, there is.

In fact, there are lots of ways that people note the difference between blowing and drawing. In this book, though, I've made it simple.

If you're supposed to blow, you'll see the number of the hole by itself.

For example, if you are supposed to play a C note, which is the 4 blow, then you would see the number 4 by itself under the word (and note).

On the other hand, if you need to draw (or suck) a note, then the number of the hole will be proceeded by a ~ sign.

So, for example, if you are supposed to draw an F note, which is the 5 draw, it will be annotated with a ~5.

For example, let's say you want to play _Row, Row, Row Your Boat_.

Here's how the harmonica tablature would look:

> _Row, row, row, your boat._
> 4   4   4   -4   5

> _Gently down the stream._
> 5   -4   5   -5   6

> _Me-rr-ily, me-rr-ily, me-rr-ily, me-rr-ily,_
> 7   7 7 6 6 6 5 5 5 4 4 4

> _Life is but a dream._
> 6 -5 5 -4 4

Easy right?

Don't worry, you'll get it.

After a few days of playing the songs, you'll find it second nature to switch between blowing and drawing the notes.

And remember, there's no right or wrong way. Just pick up your harp and play. Make her sing. When you do, you'll find that you'll have the power to make those around you happy.

Now, time to play some gospel tunes!

Gospel Tunes

1. A Better Day Coming
2. A Friend Indeed
3. A Home Forever There
4. A Home On High
5. A Joy In My Heart
6. A Soldier Of The Cross
7. Abide With Me
8. Able To Deliver
9. All Glory Be Thine
10. All Glory Laud And Honor
11. All Glory To Thee
12. All My Journey
13. All The Way My Savior Leads Me
14. Always With Us
15. Amazing Grace
16. Anchored
17. Are You Laying Up Your Treasure
18. Are You Washed In The Blood
19. Arise And Shine
20. Asking Thy Care
21. Be Slow To Speak
22. Be Still, My Soul
23. Be Still
24. Be Thou Exalted
25. Be Faithful Unto Death
26. Beautiful City Of Gold
27. Behold The Saviour
28. Believe And Obey
29. Bless Me Now
30. Bless Me Now
31. Blessed Are The Undefiled In Heart

A Better Day Coming

Grace Weiser Davis

A Friend Indeed

J. B. MacKay

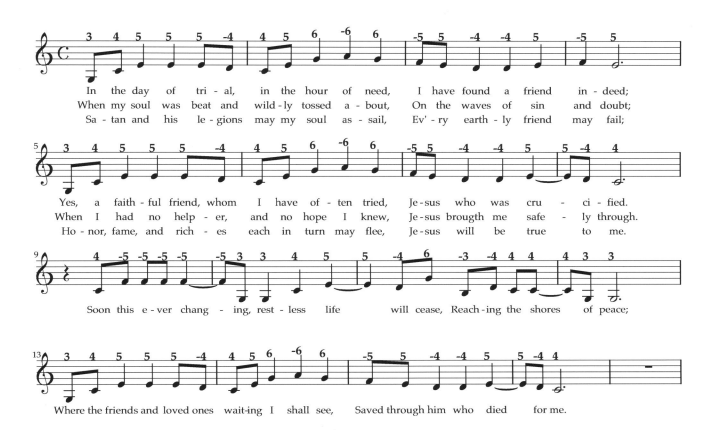

In the day of tri - al, in the hour of need, I have found a friend in - deed;
When my soul was beat and wild - ly tossed a - bout, On the waves of sin and doubt;
Sa - tan and his le - gions may my soul as - sail, Ev' - ry earth - ly friend may fail;

Yes, a faith - ful friend, whom I have of - ten tried, Je - sus who was cru - ci - fied.
When I had no help - er, and no hope I knew, Je - sus brougth me safe - ly through.
Ho - nor, fame, and rich - es each in turn may flee, Je - sus will be true to me.

Soon this e - ver chang - ing, rest - less life will cease, Reach - ing the shores of peace;

Where the friends and loved ones wait-ing I shall see, Saved through him who died for me.

A Home Forever There

Fanny Crosby

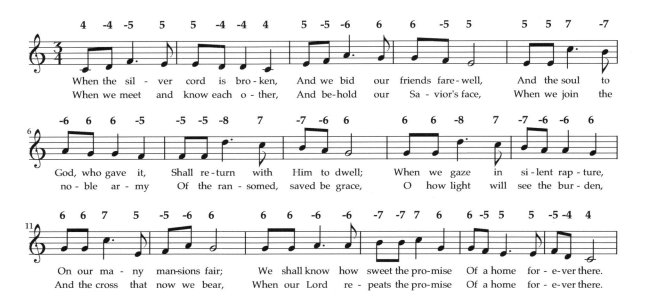

When the sil - ver cord is bro - ken, And we bid our friends fare - well, And the soul to
When we meet and know each o - ther, And be - hold our Sa - vior's face, When we join the

God, who gave it, Shall re - turn with Him to dwell; When we gaze in si - lent rap - ture,
no - ble ar - my Of the ran - somed, saved be grace, O how light will see the bur - den,

On our ma - ny man - sions fair; We shall know how sweet the pro - mise Of a home for - e - ver there.
And the cross that now we bear, When our Lord re - peats the pro - mise Of a home for - e - ver there.

A Home On High

Tom C. Neal

Tom C. Neal

A Joy In My Heart

Katharine E. Purvis

James M. Black

A Soldier Of The Cross

Isaac Watts

Abide With Me

Emma G. Dietrick

Charles Edward Pollock

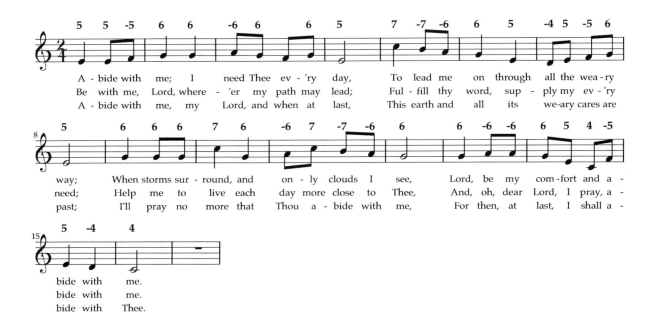

Able To Deliver

Fanny Crosby

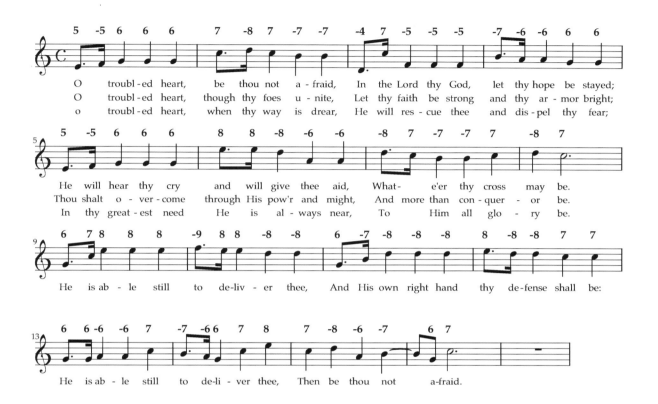

All Glory Be Thine

Fanny Crosby

All Glory Laud And Honor

Theodulph of Orleans

Melchior Teschner

All Glory To Thee

R. N. Turner

John H. Kurzenknabe

All glo - ry at - tend Thee, All prai - ses be Thine; Thou Prince of the peo - ple,
Su - preme in Thy wis - dom, E - ter - nal in might, We bow in Thy pre - sence,
O joy be - yond mea - sure, O swee - test and best; Through pa - tient en - du - rance,
Im - mor - tal Thou li - vest, We live at Thy side; Through a - ges un - en - ding,

In - car - nate Di - vine. All glo - ry and ho - nor, All bles - sings and praise; To crown Thee
O in - fi - nite Light.
We'll taste of Thy rest.
With Thee we a - bide.

fo - re - ver, Our voi - ces we raise; All glo - ry at - tend Thee, all prai - ses be Thine;

Though Prince of the peo - ple, In - car - nate Di - vine.

All My Journey

Fanny Crosby

Hart P. Danks

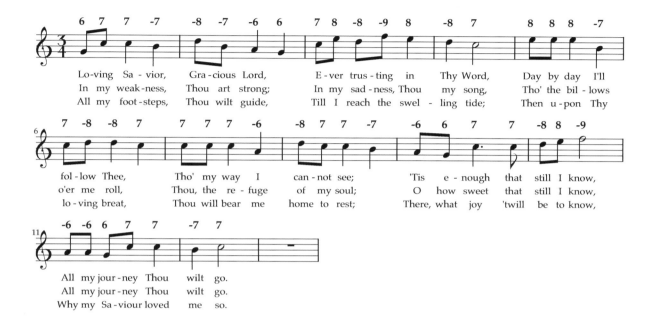

Lo-ving Sa - vior, Gra - cious Lord, E - ver trus - ting in Thy Word, Day by day I'll
In my weak-ness, Thou art strong; In my sad - ness, Thou my song, Tho' the bil - lows
All my foot-steps, Thou wilt guide, Till I reach the swel - ling tide; Then u -pon Thy

fol - low Thee, Tho' my way I can - not see; 'Tis e - nough that still I know,
o'er me roll, Thou, the re - fuge of my soul; O how sweet that still I know,
lo - ving breat, Thou will bear me home to rest; There, what joy 'twill be to know,

All my jour -ney Thou wilt go.
All my jour -ney Thou wilt go.
Why my Sa -viour loved me so.

All The Way My Savior Leads Me

Fanny J. Crosby

Robert Lowry

Always With Us

Edwin H. Nevin

T.C. O'Kane

Al - ways with us, al - ways with us, Words of cheer, and words of love; Thus the ri - sen
With us when the storm is sweep-ing, O'er are path - way dark and drear; Wak-ing hope with -

Sa-vior whis-pers, From His dwel-ling place a - bove. With us when we toil in sad - ness,
in our bo - soms, Still - ing ev - v'ry anx - ious fear. With us in the lone ly val - ley,

Sew - ing much, and reap-ing none; Tell-ing us that in the fu - ture Gol - den har-vests shall
When we cross the chill-ing stream; Light-ing up the steps to glo - ry With sal - va -tion's ra -

be won.
di ant beam.

Amazing Grace

John Newton

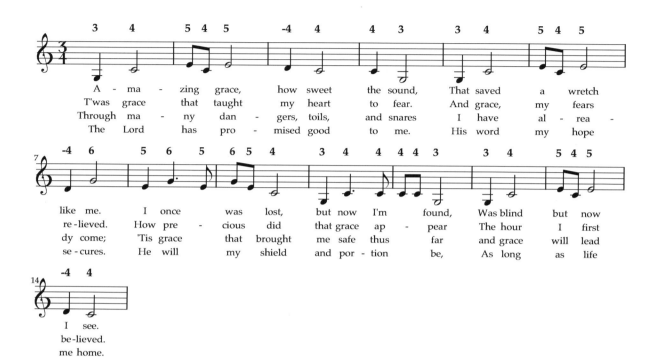

Anchored

Clara M. Brooks

Barney E. Warren

Long my rest - less soul had sought Re - fuge from the troub - led sea;
As my spi - rit ter - ror filled, Breas - ted storm and tide a - lone,
Je - sus Mas - ter of the sea, Ne - ver let my ves - sel strand;
Safe - ly by the rock - bound coast, And the treach - 'rous break - ers past,

Strug - gling vain - ly till I thought There was no re - pose for me;
Je - sus came, the tem - pest stilled, Hushed its loud and ang - ry moan;
Keep me shel - tered in the lee, In the hol - low of Thy hand,
Guide me, lest my way be lost, In - to heav - en's port at last.

Je - sus whis - pered 'mid the storm, "Trust Mine e - ver - last - ing arm."
Stan - ding on the rest - less wave, Reached His hand my sould to save.
Free from storm and tem - pest shock, An - chored deep - ly in the rock.
Stor - my seas no more I'll sail, Safe at last with - in the veil.

Trust Mine e - ver - last - ing arm."
Reached His hand my soul to save.
An - chored deepl - ly in the rock.
Safe at last with - in the veil.

Are You Laying Up Your Treasure

Julia Johnston

Daniel B. Towner

Are you lay-ing up your trea - sure, Where no moth nor rust can e - ver spoil?
Here on earth are scat-tered je - wels, Je - wels that may shine for - e - ver-more;
Pre - cious souls may be your trea - sure, Gifts of love and deeds of mer - cy shown,
With your trea - sure will your heart be, Are your pre - cious stores laid up on high?

What shall be the fi - nal mea - sure, What shall be the gain of ear - thly toil?
In the Sa - vior's crown of glo - ry, Will you ga - ther these for yon bright shore?
These may go be - fore to meet you, When the Lord of life calls go - ing by.
Then your life is rich - er grow - ing, While the hast -'ning days are go - ing by.

Lay - ing up your trea - sure, Heap-ing up the mea - sure In the safe and sec - ret place a - bove.

Glad - ly, glad - ly shall we find it, In the realms of light and joy and love.

Are You Washed In The Blood

Elisha A. Hoffman

Elisha A. Hoffman

Arise And Shine

Carrie E. Breck

Daniel B. Towner

Asking Thy Care

G. A. Sanders

D. F. Hodges

Dear Sa - vior! The bat - tle of life is so great, It's bur - dens for me are
My hope is in Thee, Thou de - sire of my soul, My trust and af - fec - tions
Ah, streng - then my cou - rage, my spi - rit now cheer, Life's path - ways so cloud - y,

too hea - vy to bear; I come, for with Thee it is ne - ver too late,
shall none o - ther share; To Thee ev - er com - ing, My life now con - trol,
make bright, plain and clear; Now help me to tra - vel with Thee e - ver near,

With faith and with con - fi - dence ask - ing Thy care. Ask - ing Thy care, Ask - ing
With faith and with con - fi - dence ask - ing Thy care.
In faith and in con - fi - dence ask - ing Thy care.

Thy care, With faith and with con - fi - dence Ask - ing Thy care.

Be Slow to Speak

Kate Ulmer

Be Still, My Soul

Kathrina von Schlegel

Be Still

Kate Ulmer

Charles C. Ackley

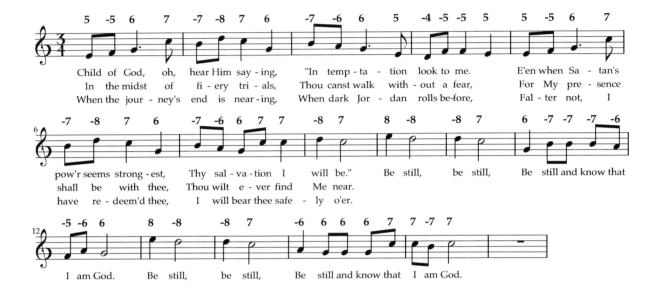

Child of God, oh, hear Him say - ing, "In temp - ta - tion look to me. E'en when Sa - tan's
In the midst of fi - ery tri - als, Thou canst walk with - out a fear, For My pre - sence
When the jour - ney's end is near - ing, When dark Jor - dan rolls be-fore, Fal - ter not, I

pow'r seems strong - est, Thy sal - va - tion I will be." Be still, be still, Be still and know that
shall be with thee, Thou wilt e - ver find Me near.
have re - deem'd thee, I will bear thee safe - ly o'er.

I am God. Be still, be still, Be still and know that I am God.

Be Thou Exalted

Fanny Crosby

John S. Farris

Be Thou Faithful Unto Death

Anonymous

Beautiful City of Gold

I.N. McHose

Behold The Saviour

Alice Jean Cleator

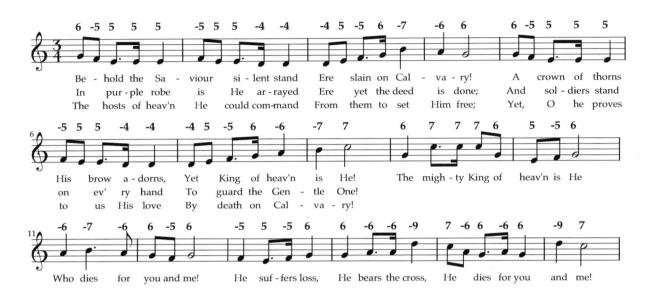

Be - hold the Sa - viour si - lent stand   Ere   slain on Cal - va - ry!   A   crown of thorns
In   pur - ple robe   is   He ar - rayed   Ere   yet the deed   is   done;   And   sol - diers stand
The   hosts of heav'n   He   could com-mand   From   them to set   Him free;   Yet,   O   he proves

His   brow a - dorns,   Yet   King   of heav'n   is   He!   The   migh - ty King of   heav'n is He
on   ev' ry hand   To   guard the Gen - tle   One!
to   us   His love   By   death on Cal - va - ry!

Who dies   for   you and me!   He   suf - fers loss,   He   bears the cross,   He   dies for you   and me!

Believe And Obey

Fanny Crosby

Press on - ward, press on - ward, and trust - ing the Lord, Re - mem - ber the pro - mise
Press on - ward, press on - ward, if you would se - cure The rest of the faith - ful,
Press on - ward, press on - ward, your cour - age re - new; The prize is be - fore you,

pro-claimed in His Word; He guid -eth the foot - steps, di - rect - eth the way Of all who
a - bid - ing and sure; The gift of sal - va - tion is of -fered to - day To all who
the crown is in view; His love is so bound -less, He'll ne - ver say nay To those who

con - fess Him, be - lieve, and o - bey. Be - lieve and o - bey, be - lieve and o - bey;
con - fess Him, be - lieve, and o - bey.
con - fess Him, be - lieve, and o - bey.

The Mas - ter is call - ing, no long - er de - lay. The light of His mer - cy shines bright on

the way Of all who con - fess Him, be - lieve, and o - bey.

Bless Me Now

Alexander Clark

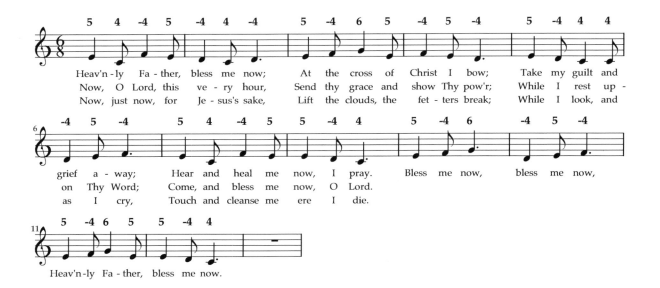

Heav'n-ly Fa - ther, bless me now; At the cross of Christ I bow; Take my guilt and
Now, O Lord, this ve - ry hour, Send thy grace and show Thy pow'r; While I rest up -
Now, just now, for Je - sus's sake, Lift the clouds, the fet - ters break; While I look, and

grief a - way; Hear and heal me now, I pray. Bless me now, bless me now,
on Thy Word; Come, and bless me now, O Lord.
as I cry, Touch and cleanse me ere I die.

Heav'n-ly Fa - ther, bless me now.

Bless Me Now

Alexander Clark

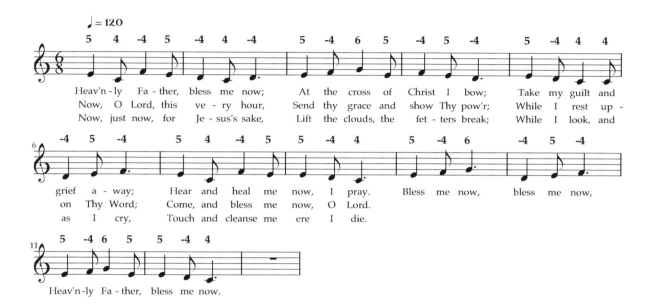

Heav'n-ly Fa - ther, bless me now; At the cross of Christ I bow; Take my guilt and
Now, O Lord, this ve - ry hour, Send thy grace and show Thy pow'r; While I rest up -
Now, just now, for Je - sus's sake, Lift the clouds, the fet - ters break; While I look, and

grief a - way; Hear and heal me now, I pray. Bless me now, bless me now,
on Thy Word; Come, and bless me now, O Lord.
as I cry, Touch and cleanse me ere I die.

Heav'n-ly Fa - ther, bless me now.

Blessed Are The Undefiled In Heart

Isaac Watts

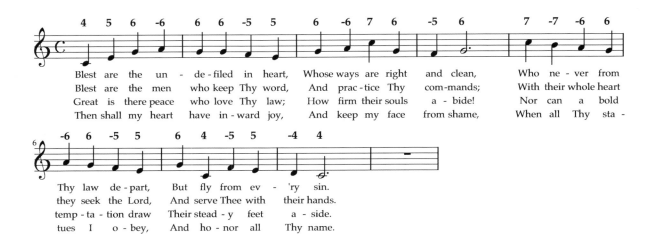

Blest are the un - de - filed in heart, Whose ways are right and clean, Who ne - ver from
Blest are the men who keep Thy word, And prac - tice Thy com - mands; With their whole heart
Great is there peace who love Thy law; How firm their souls a - bide! Nor can a bold
Then shall my heart have in - ward joy, And keep my face from shame, When all Thy sta -

Thy law de - part, But fly from ev - 'ry sin.
they seek the Lord, And serve Thee with their hands.
temp - ta - tion draw Their stead - y feet a - side.
tues I o - bey, And ho - nor all Thy name.

Blessed Assurance

Fanny J. Crosby

Bless-ed as-su-rance, Je-sus is mine! Oh, what a fore-taste of glo-ry-di-vine!
Per-fect sub-mis-sion, per-fect de-light, Vi-sions of rap-ture now burst on my sight;
Per-fect sub-mis-sion, all is at rest, I in my Sav-iour am hap-py and blest;

Heir of sal-va-tion, pur-chase of God, Born of His spi-rit, washed in His blood.
Ang-els de-scend-ing, bring from a-bove E-choes of mer-cy, whis-pers of love.
Watch-ing and wait-ing, look-ing a-bove, Filled with His good-ness, lost in His love.

This is my sto-ry, this is my song, Prais-ing my Sa-viour all the day long;

This is my sto-ry, this is my song, Prais-ing my Sa-viour all the day long.

Blessed Communion

Burton H. Winslow

Blessed Rock

Fanny Crosby

'Mid the wild and fear - ful blast, I have reached the Rock at last;
Wrecked by sin, by tem - pest tossed, Com-pass, chart and an - chor lost;
Rock, that hides my tremb - ling soul, From the storms that dark - ly roll;

Help - less, weak and sore dis-mayed, To the cross I'll cling for aid.
He whose pow'r a - lone can save, Lulls the wind and stills the wave.
While be - neath the sur - ges dash Thun-ders roar, and light - nings flash.

Bless - ed "Rock," whose love di - vine, Fills with joy this heart of mine;

Cross of Him who died for me, Ev - er-more I'll cling to Thee.

Breathe On Me, Breath of God

Edwin Hatch

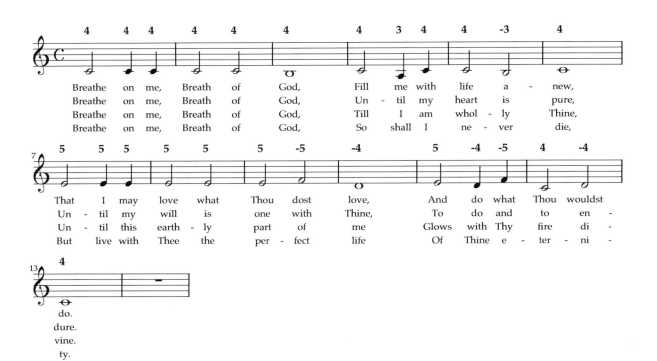

Breathe on me, Breath of God, Fill me with life a - new,
Breathe on me, Breath of God, Un - til my heart is pure,
Breathe on me, Breath of God, Till I am whol - ly Thine,
Breathe on me, Breath of God, So shall I ne - ver die,

That I may love what Thou dost love, And do what Thou wouldst
Un - til my will is one with Thine, To do and to en -
Un - til this earth - ly part of me Glows with Thy fire di -
But live with Thee the per - fect life Of Thine e - ter - ni -

do.
dure.
vine.
ty.

Can You Stand For God

Horace L. Hastings

Can you stand for God, though you stand a - lone, With your heart at rest, and your soul se - cure,
Can you stand for God, when the heart grows faint, And your soul looks through ma - ny blind-ing tears,
Can you stand with faith, though the time be long, Though the night be dark and the day star dim,

With the rock be - neath and in front the throne, Can you stand and still en - dure?
Can you bear life's sor - rows with - out comp - laint Through te - di - ous toil - some years?
Can you stand for truth and in Christ be strong, Till you stand comp - lete in Him?

Can you stand, can you stand, Can you stand for Christ a - lone? If we stand in the strife,

till the end of life, We shall stand at the heav'n - ly throne.

Carry It All To Jesus

H. J. Zelley

Christ The Light

Harriet Pierson

When the clouds ga - ther thick - ly and the sha - dows lie Dark and deep a - cross the way,
For the feet that have wand -ered from the path as - tray, Lost in ma - zes dark and wild,
O'er the hills comes the dawn -ing, with its ra - diance bright; 'Tis the Sun of Right -eous -ness

We must tread from day to day, There's a light to cheer us; lo it gleams on high
By the lure of sin be - guiled, Still the Day - star is point - ing to the shin - ing way,
Come to heal a world's dis - tress; Soon His rays will il - lu - mine all the earth's dark night

Like a bea - con in the mid - night sky. See the light shin - ing clear!
Lead -ing up -ward to the gates of day.
With a glo - ry from the heav - 'nly height.

'Tis the Christ that our long -ing eyes be -hold; He will lead us on till the night is gone;

And the splend -ors of the morn un - fold.

City Of Gold

Fanny Crosby

There's a ci - ty that looks o'er the val - ley of death, And the glo - ries can ne - ver be told;
There the King, our Re - dee - mer, the Lord whom we love, All the faith - ful with rap - ture be-hold;
Ev - 'ry soul we have led to the foot of the cross, Ev - 'ry lamb we have brought to the fold,

There the sun ne - ver sets and the leaves ne-ver fade, In that beau-ti - ful ci - ty of gold.
There the right-eous for - e - ver shall shine as the stars, In that beau-ti - ful ci - ty of gold.
Shall be kept as bright je - wels our crown to a - dorn, In that beau-ti - ful ci - ty of gold.

There the sun ne - ver sets, and the leaves ne - ver fade; And the eyes of the faith -

ful our Sa - vior be-hold, In that beau-ti - ful ci - ty of gold.

Cleanse Thou Me

Fanny Crosby

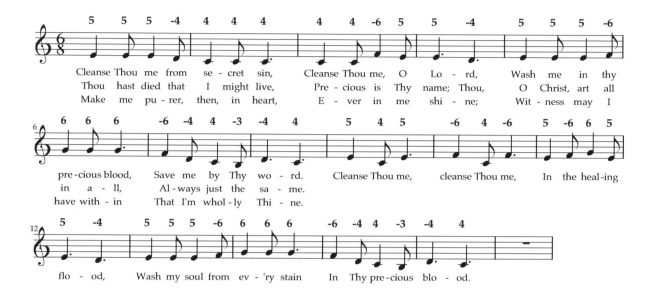

Close To Thee

Fanny Crosby

Thou my e - ver - last - ing por - tion, more than friend or life to me, all a - long my
Not for ease or world - ly plea - sure, nor for fame my prayer shall be; glad - ly will I
Lead my through the vale of sha - dows, bear me o'er life's fit - ful sea; then the gate of

pil - grim jour - ney, Sa - vior, let me walk with thee. Close to thee, close to thee,
toil and suf - fer, on - ly let me walk with thee.
life e - ter - nal may I en - ter, Lord, with thee.

close to thee, close to thee, all - a-long my pil -grim jour -ney, Sa-vior, let me walk with thee.

Closer Draw Me

Kate Ulmer

Closer To Jesus

Rufus H. McDaniel

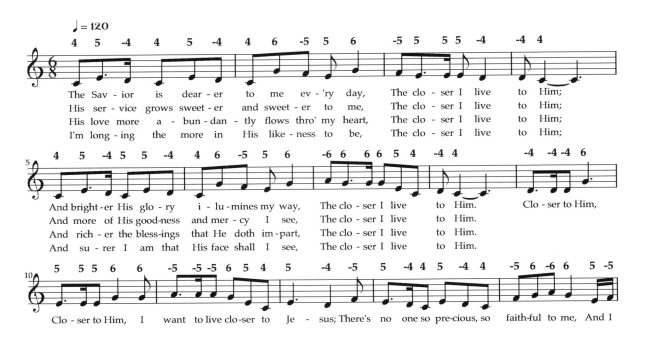

Closer to Thee, Blessed Saviour

John H. Kurzenknabe

Clo - ser to Thee, bless-ed Sa - viour, Take me and shel - ter me there;
Clo - ser to Thee, bless-ed Sa - viour, In Thy strong arms may I hide;
Clo - ser to Thee, bless-ed Sa - viour, Lean - ing on Thy ten - der breast,

Like as the faint droop - ing li - lies, I need Thy ten - der - est - care.
Keep me from sin and temp - ta - tion, E - ver with Thee to a - bide.
Take me, Thou pre - cious Re - dee - mer, Here let my soul sweet - ly rest.

Clo - ser to Thee, bless-ed Sa - viour to Thee, Clo-ser, still clo-ser, still clo-ser to Thee.

Come And Sin No more

Grant C. Tullar

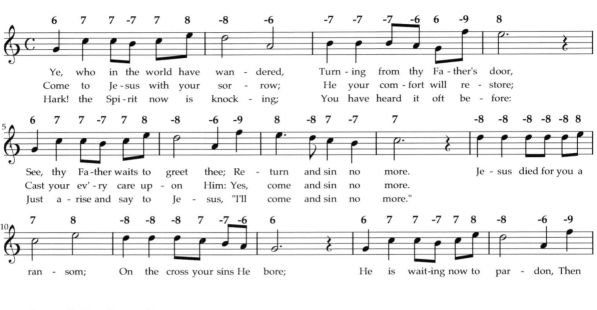

Ye, who in the world have wan - dered, Turn - ing from thy Fa - ther's door,
Come to Je - sus with your sor - row; He your com - fort will re - store;
Hark! the Spi - rit now is knock - ing; You have heard it oft be - fore:

See, thy Fa - ther waits to greet thee; Re - turn and sin no more. Je - sus died for you a
Cast your ev' - ry care up - on Him: Yes, come and sin no more.
Just a - rise and say to Je - sus, "I'll come and sin no more."

ran - som; On the cross your sins He bore; He is wait-ing now to par - don, Then

come and sin no more.

Come Just As You Are

Elisha A. Hoffman

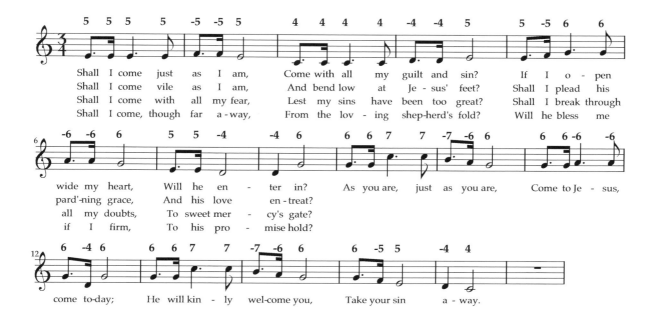

Shall I come just as I am, Come with all my guilt and sin? If I o - pen
Shall I come vile as I am, And bend low at Je - sus' feet? Shall I plead his
Shall I come with all my fear, Lest my sins have been too great? Shall I break through
Shall I come, though far a - way, From the lov - ing shep-herd's fold? Will he bless me

wide my heart, Will he en - ter in? As you are, just as you are, Come to Je - sus,
pard'-ning grace, And his love en - treat?
all my doubts, To sweet mer - cy's gate?
if I firm, To his pro - mise hold?

come to-day; He will kin - ly wel-come you, Take your sin a - way.

Come To Christ Today

W. Bennett

Come to Je - sus, pre - cious soul, Come to Je - sus, come to Je - sus;
Come to Je - sus, doubt - ing heart, Come to Je - sus, come to Je - sus;
Come to Je - sus, don't de - lay, Come to Je - sus, come to Je - sus;

He will make the wound - ed whole, Come, O come to - day; He will wash you
Bid your un - be - lief de - part, Trust his word to - day; Faith us strong and
Come to Je - sus while you may, Come, O come to - day; Let his love your

in his blood, Free - ly flows the cleans-ing flood; He will take your sins a - way,
must pre - vail, Come with faith you can - not fail; All your doubts and fears shall fly;
hearts con-strain, Do not let him plead in vain; He hath died up - on the tree,

Come, O come to Christ to - day.
Faith tri - um - phant mounts the sky.
Shed his pre - cious blood for thee.

Come To The Living Waters

J. H. Alleman

Come to the liv-ing wat-ers! Why will ye thir-sty be? The fount-ain of
Come to the liv-ing wat-ers! Come now, no long-er wait! His spi-rit with
Come to the liv-ing wat-ers! Come who-so-ev-er will! To-day hear the
Come to the liv-ing wat-ers! From ev-er flow-ing main; Come drink and have

life is flow-ing, Is flow-ing now for thee. He who-so-ev-er will may come, And
thine is striv-ing, Come ere it be too late.
in-vi-ta-tion, That ev'-ry soul should thrill.
life e-ter-nal, And ne-ver thirst a-gain.

take of the wat-er of life free-ly; He who-so-ev-er will may come, And

take of the wat-er, the wat-er of life.

Come Unto Me

Lizzie Ashbach

Come un - to me, the Sav - iour said, And be for - e -
Take up my yoke, it shall be light, I'll bear a part
For I, the high and ho - ly one, Was meek and low -
All my com - mands o - bey and thou Shalt be my hon -

ver blest; Come, all ye wear - y ones come near, And I will give
for thee; Come, fol - low in the steps I tread, And meek - ly learn
ly, too; With rev' - rence come and learn of me, My pre - cepts keep
ored guest; Par - don and peace shall here be thine, And there e - ter -

you rest. Come un - to me, ye wear - y, come, And I will give
of me.
in view.
nal rest.

you rest; Come take my yoke and learn of me, And be for - e -

ver blest.

Come, Prodigal, Come

W. A. Ogden

The foun - tain of   sal - va - tion   Is flow - ing full   and free,   And Je - sus stands
I   hear his cry   "Tis fin - ished,"   His bleed -ing bo - dy see,   His lo - ving ac -
His bless -ed in - vi - ta - tion   I will no long - er spurn,   And from my great

in - vi - ting: Oh, sin - ner come   to me.   I hear his sweet   voice plead - ing.
cents thrills   me.   His bless - ed "Come   to me."
ex - am - ple   I will no long - er turn.

For me tis in - ter - ce - ding.   The way   I know,   And I   will go,   My Sa - viour calls   for me.

Come, pro - di - gal, come,   While yet   there's room.   Come, pro - di - gal, come,

Thy Sa - viour call - eth thee.

Committed To Jesus

Minnie B. Johnson

Com-mit-ted to Je - sus, my-self and my all, To do at His bid - ding
Com-mit-ted to Je - sus, my-ev - 'ry-day life; Well know-ing it means for
Com-mit-ted to Je - sus, my in - ner-most will, My in - ner-most pur - pose,

and go at His call; A work-er in earn - est, both faith-ful and true,
me con-flict and strife; To faith-ful-ly do all the will of the Lord,
His wish to ful-fill; With ar - dor, His ser - vice, I'll ev - er pur-sue,

With-hold-ing no ser - vice my weak hand can do. Com-mit-ted to Je - sus,
And fol - low Him ful - ly, o - bey - ing His word.
And do what-so-ev - er He bids me to do.

my bo-dy and soul; My gifts and pos-ses - sions, I give Him the whole;

Oh, praise the dear Sav - iour, who spoke me for - giv'n, An heir of sal - va - tion,

a pil-grim for Heav'n.

Day By Day

Karolina W Sandell-Berg

Do You Love The World

Clarence E. Hunter

Draw Me Still Closer

Frank M. Davis

Dwell In Me O Blessed Spirit

Martha J. Lankton (pseudonym of Fanny Crosby)

Dwell in me,   O   bless-ed spir - it   How I need Thy   help di - vine!   In the way   of
Let me feel   Thy   sac - red pres-ence;   Then my faith will   ne'er dec - line;   Com-fort Thou   and
Round the cross   where   Thou hast led me,   Let my pur - est   feel - ings twine;   With the blood   from
Dwell in me,   O   bless-ed spir - it,   Grac-ious Teach - er,   Friend div - ine,   For the home   of

life e - ter - nal,   Keep, oh, keep   this heart of mine.   Dwell in me,   oh,   dwell in me;
help me   on - ward,   Fill with love   this heart of mine.
sin that cleansed me,   Seal a - new   this heart of mine.
bliss that waits   me   O pre - pare   this heart of mine.

Hear and grant   my   prayer to thee;   Spir-it, now   from   heav'n des-cen - ding,   Come, oh, come   and

dwell in me.

Eternity

Will L. Thompson

Ever Near

Ellen M. Hastings

Ever Will I Pray

A. Cummings

Fath - er in the morn-ing Un - to thee I pray, Let thy lov - ing kind-ness Keep my
At the bu - sy noon-tide, Press'd with work and care, Then I'll wait with Je - sus Till he
When the eve-ning shad-ows Chase a - way the light, Fath - er then I'll pray thee, Bless thy
Thus in life's glad morn-ing, In its bright noon - day, In the shad-ow eve-ning, Ev - er

thro' this day. I will pray, I will pray, Ev - er will I pray, Morn - ing, noon, and
hears my prayer.
child to - night.
will I pray.

eve -ning Un - to thee I'll pray.

Faith Of Our Fathers

Frederick W. Faber

Faith	of	our	fath	-	ers,	liv	-	ing	still	In	spite	of	dun	-	geon,
Our	fath - ers,	chained			in	pri	-	sons	dark,	Were	still	in	heart	and
Faith	of	our	fath	-	ers,	we		will	strive	To	win	all	na	-	tions
Faith	of	our	fath	-	ers,	we		will	love	Both	friend	and	foe	in

fire,	and	sword,	O	how	our	hearts	beat	high	with	joy
cons	-	cience	free;	And	blest	would	be	their	child	-	ren's	fate,
un	-	to	thee;	And	through	the	truth	that	comes	from	God
all	our	strife,	And	preach	thee,	too,	as	love	knows	how

When - e'er	we	hear	that	glo	-	ri	-	ous	word!	Faith	of	our	fa	-	thers!	Ho	-	ly
If	they,	like	them	should	die	for	thee:
Man - kind	shall	then	in	-	deed	be	free.
By	kind - ly	words	and	vir	tu	-	ous	life.

| faith! | We | will | be | true | to | thee | till | death! |

Father To Thee

C. I. Stacey

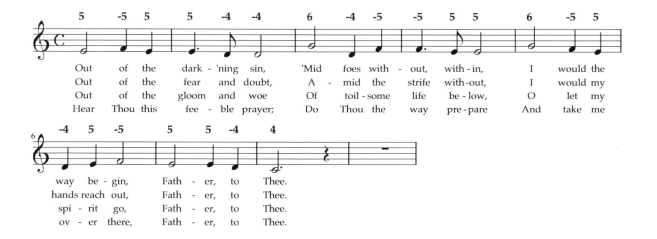

5	-5	5		5	-4	-4		6	-4	-5		-5	5	5

Out of the dark - 'ning sin, 'Mid foes with - out, with - in, I would the
Out of the fear and doubt, A - mid the strife with-out, I would my
Out of the gloom and woe Of toil - some life be - low, O let my
Hear Thou this fee - ble prayer; Do Thou the way pre - pare And take me

-4	5	-5		5	5	-4		4

way be - gin, Fath - er, to Thee.
hands reach out, Fath - er, to Thee.
spi - rit go, Fath - er, to Thee.
ov - er there, Fath - er, to Thee.

Follow In The Steps Of Jesus

Kate Ulmer

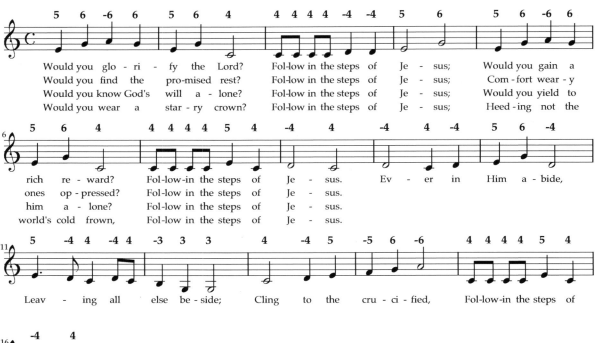

Would you glo - ri - fy the Lord? Fol-low in the steps of Je - sus; Would you gain a
Would you find the pro-mised rest? Fol-low in the steps of Je - sus; Com - fort wear - y
Would you know God's will a - lone? Fol-low in the steps of Je - sus; Would you yield to
Would you wear a star - ry crown? Fol-low in the steps of Je - sus; Heed - ing not the

rich re - ward? Fol-low in the steps of Je - sus. Ev - er in Him a - bide,
ones op - pressed? Fol-low in the steps of Je - sus.
him a - lone? Fol-low in the steps of Je - sus.
world's cold frown, Fol-low in the steps of Je - sus.

Leav - ing all else be - side; Cling to the cru - ci - fied, Fol-low-in the steps of

Je - sus.

Following Him

Charles M. Fillmore

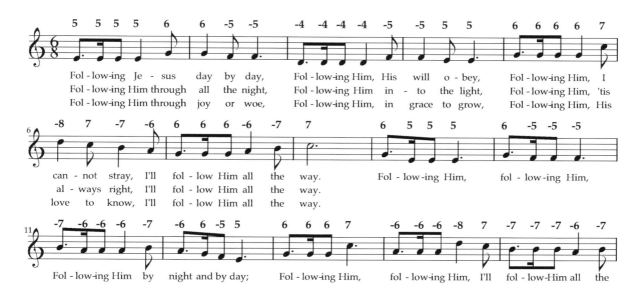

For He Careth For You

H. B. Bengle

For You And Me

Fanny Crosby

O love di - vine, a - maz - ing love! That brought to earth, from heav'n a - bove;
For us the crown of thorns he bore; For us to robe of scorn He wore;
O wond'-rer, come, on Him be -lieve, His of - fer'd grace by faith re - ceive;

The Son of God, for us to die, That we might dwell with Him on high.
He con - quered death, and rent the grave, And lives a - gain our souls to save.
A - wake, a - rise, and hear him call, The feast is spread, there's room for all.

He died for you, He died for me, And shed His blood to make us free;

Up-on the cross of Cal-va - ry, The Sav-iour died for you and me.

Forever Blessed Be The Lord

Isaac Watts

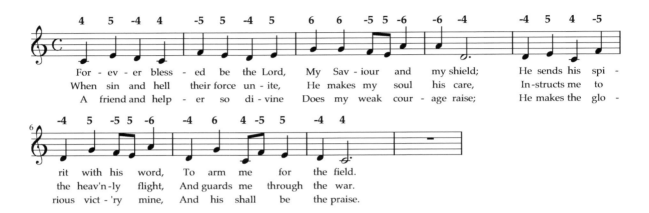

Forever With The Lord

W. H. Luckenbach

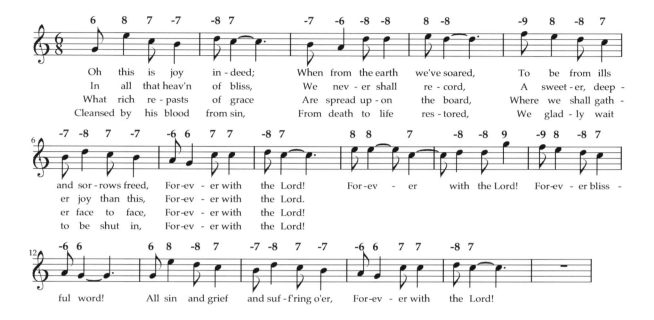

From All Who Dwell Below The Skies

Isaac Watts

From all	that dwell	be - low	the skies,	Let the	Cre - a - tors praise
E - ter - nal are	thy mer -	cies, Lord;	E - ter - nal truth	at - tends
Your lof - ty themes,	ye mor -	tals, bring,	In songs	of praise	di - vine -
In ev - 'ry land	be - gin	the song;	To ev - 'ry land	the strains

a - rise;	Let the	Re - dee - mer's name	be sung.	Through ev -
thy word.	Thy praise	shall sound	from shore	to shore,	Till suns
ly sing;	The great	sal - va - tion loud	pro - claim,	And shout
be - long;	In cheer - ful sounds	all voi -	ces raise,	And fill

'ry land	by ev - 'ry tongue.
shall rise	and set	no more.
for joy	the Sa - vior's name.
the world	with loud - est praise.

From Every Stormy Wind That Blows

Hugh Stowell

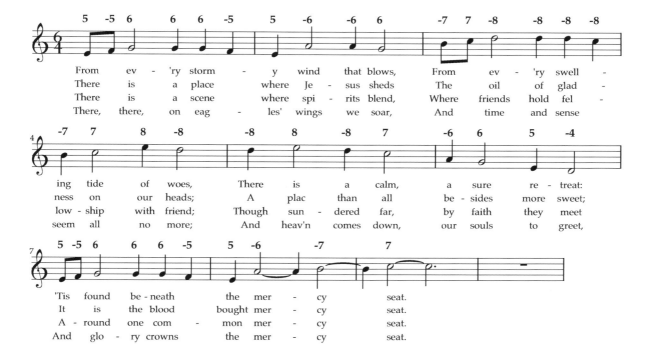

Fullness Of Joy

M. L. Herr

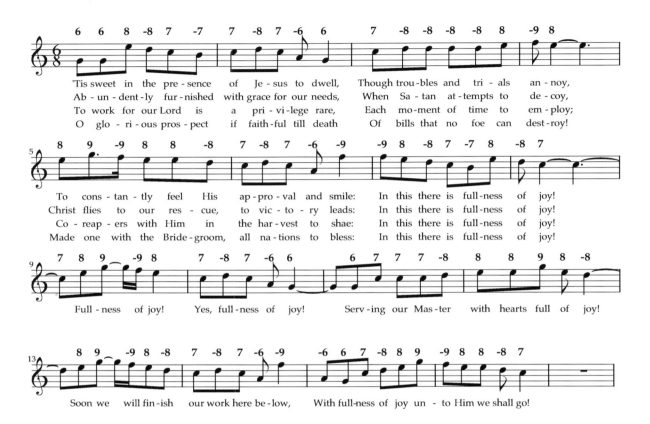

'Tis sweet in the pre - sence of Je - sus to dwell, Though trou - bles and tri - als an - noy,
Ab - un - dent - ly fur - nished with grace for our needs, When Sa - tan at - tempts to de - coy,
To work for our Lord is a pri - vi - lege rare, Each mo - ment of time to em - ploy;
O glo - ri - ous pros - pect if faith - ful till death Of bills that no foe can dest - roy!

To cons - tan - tly feel His ap - pro - val and smile: In this there is full - ness of joy!
Christ flies to our res - cue, to vic - to - ry leads: In this there is full - ness of joy!
Co - reap - ers with Him in the har - vest to shae: In this there is full - ness of joy!
Made one with the Bride - groom, all na - tions to bless: In this there is full - ness of joy!

Full - ness of joy! Yes, full - ness of joy! Serv - ing our Mas - ter with hearts full of joy!

Soon we will fin - ish our work here be - low, With full - ness of joy un - to Him we shall go!

Give Me Jesus

Fanny Crosby

Give Me Thy Love Dear Saviour

Ida L. Reed

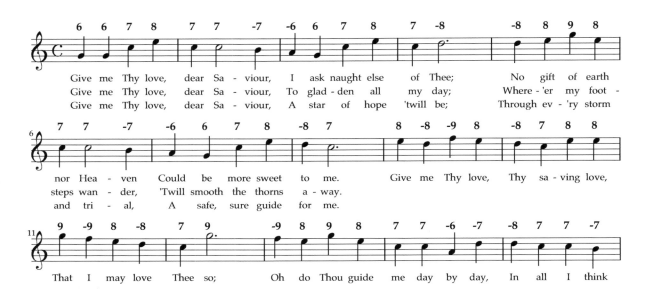

Give me Thy love, dear Sa - viour, I ask naught else of Thee;
Give me Thy love, dear Sa - viour, To glad - den all my day;
Give me Thy love, dear Sa - viour, A star of hope 'twill be;

No gift of earth
Where - 'er my foot -
Through ev - 'ry storm

nor Hea - ven Could be more sweet to me. Give me Thy love, Thy sa - ving love,
steps wan - der, 'Twill smooth the thorns a - way.
and tri - al, A safe, sure guide for me.

That I may love Thee so; Oh do Thou guide me day by day, In all I think

and do.

Glory To God, Hallelujah!

Fanny Crosby

Glory To The Bleeding Lamb

Carrie Ella Breck

Come sing a - gain the song of love, The love of God to man;
Come sing of Je - sus, wound - ed, slain, For sin - ners lost like me;
Oh worth - y worth - y is the Lamb, All glo - ry to re - ceive;
O Lord, who hast my sins for - giv'n, My joy, my song, art Thou;

The love that wrought in heav'n a - bove The great re - demp - tion plan.
He came in love to break my chains, And set the cap - tive free.
Dear Sav - ior, take me as I am, And help me now be - lieve.
I'll sing no o - ther song in heav'n, I'll sing no o - ther now.

Oh, glo - ry to the bleed - ing Lamb, For me He bled and died; I plunge be-neath

the cleans - ing blood, The foun - tain deep and wide.

God Be With You Till We Meet Again

Jeremiah E. Rankin

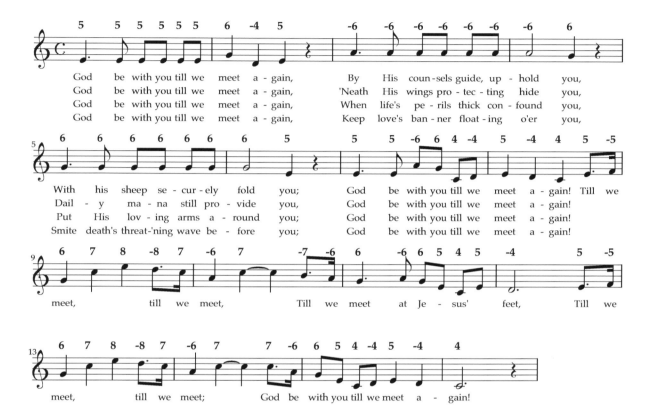

God Is Faithful

Eliza E.Hewitt

God is faith - ful, ev - er faith - ful; He will sure - ly keep his word; To the ut - ter -
God is faith - ful; he will do it; Not my own weak heart I trust, But his spi - rit
God is faith - ful, this my re - fuge; When the storms of tri - als rise; Help is com - ing,
God is faith - ful, he will make me More than con - queror in the strife; Yield-ing whol - ly

most faith - ful fill - ing Ev'ry pro - mise I have heard. God is faith - ful, ev - er faith - ful;
dwell-ing in me, Wise and ho - ly, kind and just.
swift - ly com - ing From the hills be - yond the skies.
to his guid-ance, This is bless - ing thus is life.

I will trust him all the way; God is faith - ful, ev - er faith - ful, He will keep me night and day.

God Is Present Everywhere

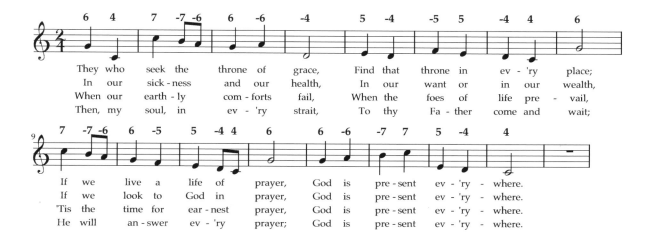

They who seek the throne of grace, Find that throne in ev - 'ry place;
In our sick - ness and our health, In our want or in our wealth,
When our earth - ly com - forts fail, When the foes of life pre - vail,
Then, my soul, in ev - 'ry strait, To thy Fa - ther come and wait;

If we live a life of prayer, God is pre - sent ev - 'ry - where.
If we look to God in prayer, God is pre - sent ev - 'ry - where.
'Tis the time for ear - nest prayer, God is pre - sent ev - 'ry - where.
He will an - swer ev - 'ry prayer; God is pre - sent ev - 'ry - where.

God Knows Thy Need

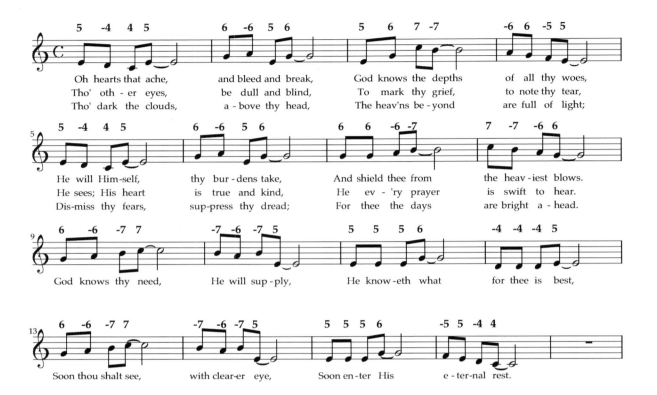

Oh hearts that ache, and bleed and break, God knows the depths of all thy woes,
Tho' oth - er eyes, be dull and blind, To mark thy grief, to note thy tear,
Tho' dark the clouds, a - bove thy head, The heav'ns be - yond are full of light;

He will Him-self, thy bur - dens take, And shield thee from the heav - iest blows.
He sees; His heart is true and kind, He ev - 'ry prayer is swift to hear.
Dis-miss thy fears, sup-press thy dread; For thee the days are bright a - head.

God knows thy need, He will sup - ply, He know - eth what for thee is best,

Soon thou shalt see, with clear-er eye, Soon en - ter His e - ter-nal rest.

God Leads Us Along

George A. Young

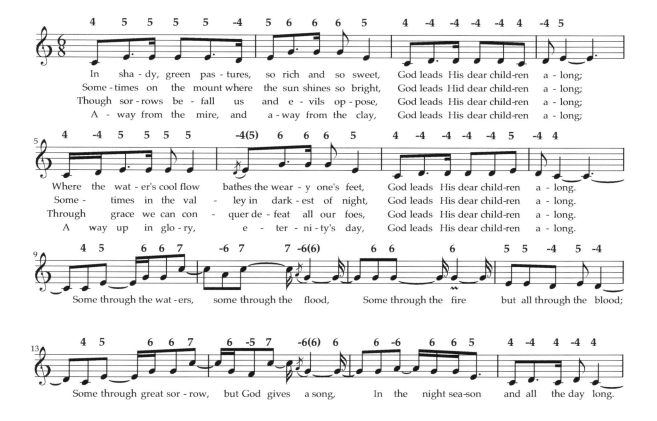

God Of Eternity

Fanny Crosby

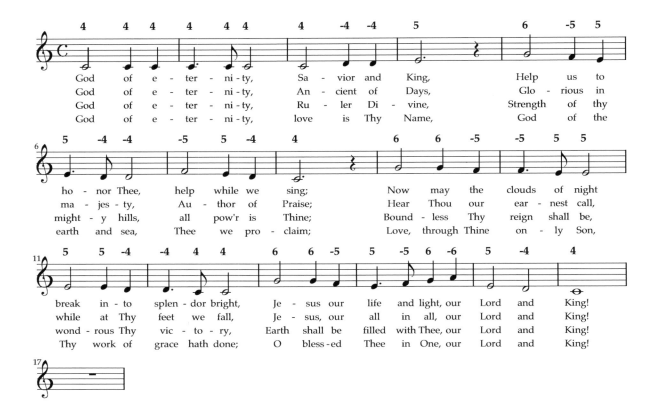

God of e - ter - ni - ty, Sa - vior and King, Help us to
God of e - ter - ni - ty, An - cient of Days, Glo - rious in
God of e - ter - ni - ty, Ru - ler Di - vine, Strength of thy
God of e - ter - ni - ty, love is Thy Name, God of the

ho - nor Thee, help while we sing; Now may the clouds of night
ma - jes - ty, Au - thor of Praise; Hear Thou our ear - nest call,
might - y hills, all pow'r is Thine; Bound - less Thy reign shall be,
earth and sea, Thee we pro - claim; Love, through Thine on - ly Son,

break in - to splen - dor bright, Je - sus our life and light, our Lord and King!
while at Thy feet we fall, Je - sus, our all in all, our Lord and King!
wond - rous Thy vic - to - ry, Earth shall be filled with Thee, our Lord and King!
Thy work of grace hath done; O bless - ed Thee in One, our Lord and King!

God The Father Almighty

Isaac Watts

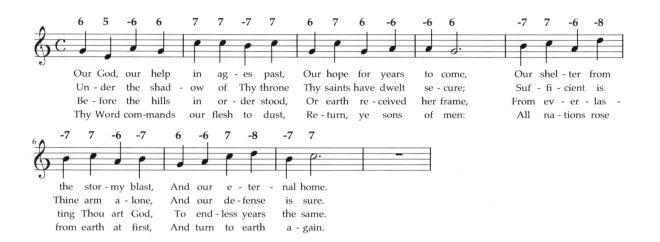

Our God, our help in ag - es past, Our hope for years to come, Our shel - ter from
Un - der the shad - ow of Thy throne Thy saints have dwelt se - cure; Suf - fi - cient is
Be - fore the hills in or - der stood, Or earth re - ceived her frame, From ev - er - las -
Thy Word com-mands our flesh to dust, Re - turn, ye sons of men: All na - tions rose

the stor - my blast, And our e - ter - nal home.
Thine arm a - lone, And our de - fense is sure.
ting Thou art God, To end - less years the same.
from earth at first, And turn to earth a - gain.

God Will Take Care Of Me

E. E. Hewitt

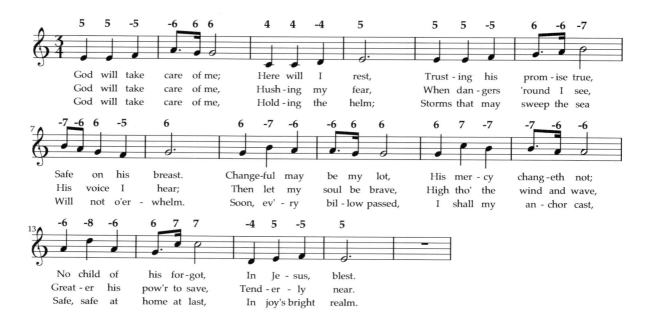

God will take care of me; Here will I rest, Trust-ing his prom-ise true,
God will take care of me, Hush-ing my fear, When dan-gers 'round I see,
God will take care of me, Hold-ing the helm; Storms that may sweep the sea

Safe on his breast. Change-ful may be my lot, His mer-cy chang-eth not;
His voice I hear; Then let my soul be brave, High tho' the wind and wave,
Will not o'er - whelm. Soon, ev'-ry bil-low passed, I shall my an-chor cast,

No child of his for-got, In Je - sus, blest.
Great - er his pow'r to save, Tend - er - ly near.
Safe, safe at home at last, In joy's bright realm.

Great Is His Mercy

Maud Frazer

I'll sing and re - joice in my Sa - viour's dear name; Great is His mer-cy to - ward me;
In all that be - falls me, I know Je - sus cares; Great is His mer-cy to - ward me;
He sought me when wand-'ring in sin's dread - ful night; Great is His mer-cy to - ward me;
Tho' oft with ne - glect this dear friend I pass'd by, Great is His mer-cy to - ward me;

And ev - er his won - der - ful love I'll pro - claim. Great is His mer-cy t'ward me.
He light - ens each bur - den, each sor - row He shares; Great is His mer-cy t'ward me.
He brought me from dark - ness to marv - e - lous light, Great is His mer-cy t'ward me.
He op - ened His arms when to Him I did cry, Great is His mer-cy t'ward me.

Great is His mer-cy t'ward me, Yes, great is his mer-cy t'ward me, He par -dons my sin,

Gives glo - ry with-in; Oh, great is His mer-cy t'ward me.

Made in the USA
Las Vegas, NV
07 April 2025